PRINCESS PIPER
of Poopville

Written by Jana Chesley
Illustrations by QBN Studios

Text copyright © 2022 by Jana Chesley

Author - Jana Chesley
Illustrator - QBN Studios
Editor - Patrina Thomas-Morrison

All rights reserved. No part of this publication, including its characters, may be reproduced or transmitted in any form or by any means, electronic or mechanical, including photocopying, recording, or by information storage and retrieval system, without written permission of the author.

Softcover ISBN - 979-8-9856804-0-9
EBook ISBN - 979-8-9856804-1-6
Hardcover ISBN: 979-8-9856804-2-3
Library of Congress Control Number: 2022902684

This book is dedicated to my amazingly creative daughters, Cora and Camille.

Princess Piper of Poopville is a kind, brave, and very smart princess. She rules over Poopville, which is a lovely place with beautiful flowers, lush green trees, and fields full of lollipop bushes.

The people of Poopville are very happy and everyone loves Princess Piper. She is always thinking of ways to make Poopville special.

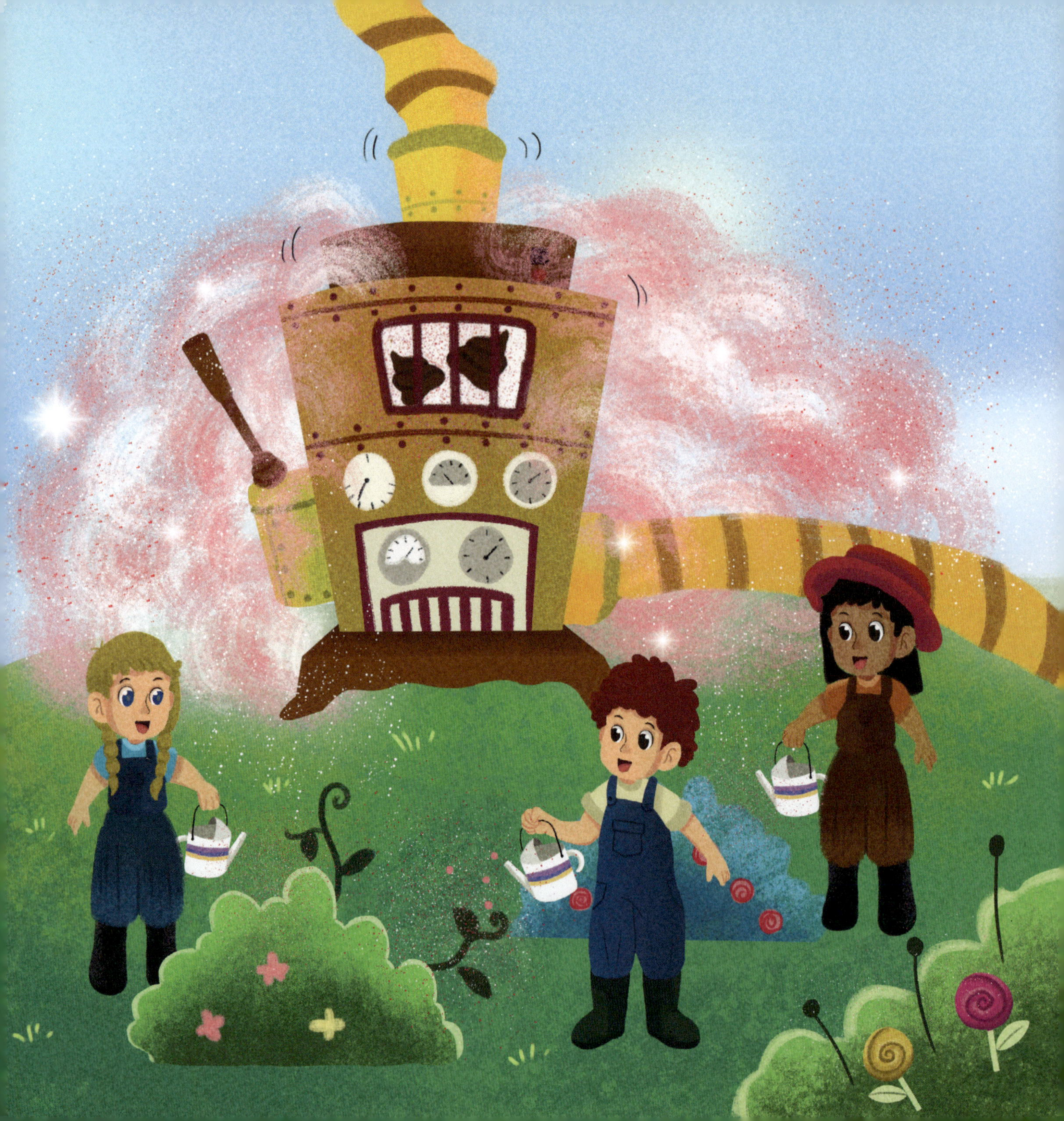

Poopville is a very important place, because it is where all the poop goes after it is flushed down the toilet. As you can imagine, all the poop was becoming a problem, so Princess Piper invented a magical machine that turns the poop into sparkly pink fairy dust.

The sparkly pink fairy dust is sprinkled on the flowers, trees, and lollipop bushes to help them grow.

Not far away, an evil queen was plotting to invade Poopville. You see, she really loved lollipops and wanted to have the lollipop bushes all to herself.

The queen and her army were on their way to attack when a tiny fairy overheard their malicious plan. The fairy flew as fast as she could to warn Princess Piper.

Thankfully, the fairy reached Princess Piper in time. Princess Piper had an idea, so she rushed to the magical poop machine.

When she got to the machine, she immediately called an emergency meeting with the people of Poopville. "We are under attack! An evil queen is coming to steal our lollipop bushes!" she exclaimed.

They knew what had to be done. Princess Piper and the people of Poopville filled their catapults with poop and launched it toward the invading army.

The poop landed in a big pile and completely blocked the invading army's path. It was so smelly that the evil queen and her army turned around and ran straight home. Princess Piper and the people of Poopville defeated the evil queen! Please remember that only Princess Piper and the people of Poopville can launch poop in a catapult!

Now, Princess Piper needs YOUR help. She would like to cordially invite you to become an official Royal Pooper. The duty of a Royal Pooper is to poop in the toilet and flush it down to Poopville every time you poop.

This is an extremely important mission, and must be taken very seriously. It ensures that the people of Poopville will always have enough poop to turn into fairy dust and sprinkle on the lollipop bushes so they continue to grow.

Princess Piper and the people of Poopville are so excited when new poop arrives that they celebrate with a song and dance.

Poop Celebration

Also, you never know when the evil queen might return to Poopville, but as long as you keep flushing your poop down the toilet, Princess Piper and the people of Poopville will be ready!

I can do this. I'm a Royal Pooper now, and Princess Piper is counting on me!

If you ever feel unsure of yourself when trying to poop in the toilet, remember that you are now an official Royal Pooper. Princess Piper believes in you, and she is counting on you. She knows that you are big, and you are brave, and you can poop in the toilet!

I am a Royal Pooper

Happy Pooping

The End

About the Author:

Jana Chesley lives right outside of Atlanta in Brookhaven, Georgia, with her husband and two daughters. Jana is a dedicated mother and community volunteer. She is very involved with local Atlanta nonprofit organizations focused on empowering women and protecting children. Jana's love for children led her to work as a substitute preschool teacher. Her favorite part about teaching was reading to the children and watching their reactions. Prior to exiting the corporate world in order to spend more time with her daughters, Jana had a ten-year career in corporate finance. This is her first children's book.

About the Illustrators:

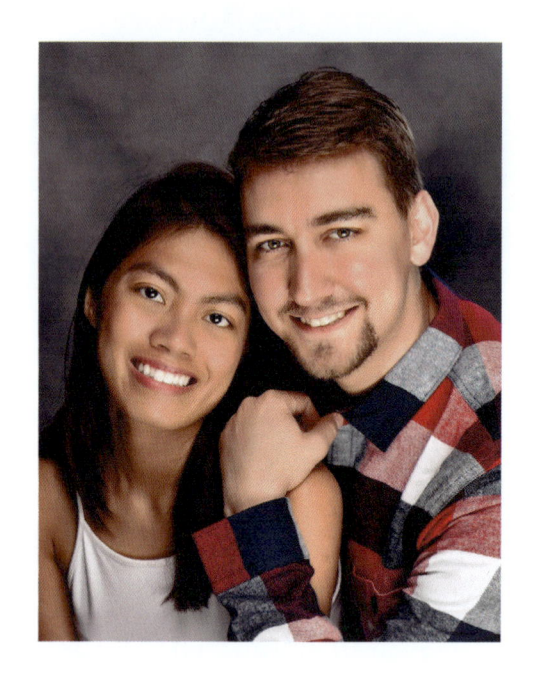

QBN Studios is a small Illustration studio located in Vernon, Connecticut. Owners Quynh Nguyen and Christopher MacCoy are passionate about helping authors fulfill their dreams and bring their words to life. QBN Studio's goal is to create an immersive experience for their audiences, to tumble headfirst into imaginary worlds. Follow us on Instagram @qbnstudios for the latest updates on illustrations, books, and other projects.